The Little One Behind The Badge

Jenny Swartout

NODIN PRESS

ISBN: 978-1-935666-95-0

published by

Nodin Press
5114 Cedar Lake Road
Minneapolis, MN 55416

Dedicated to:

My son Brenden, my husband Jake, family members, friends, and

to all the serving and fallen officers.

Acknowledgements:

Anoka County Sheriff's Department

Savage Police Department

Faithful Shepherd Catholic School

They told me he was a hero.

They told me he protected others in our town.

They told me he was kind to

all people.

They told me he keeps people safe.

I told people he was my partner

in crime.

I told people that while I put on my pajamas, he puts on his uniform.

I told people my dad cheered for me
from his squad car.

I told people that my dad told me I was man of the house as he kissed us good-bye for the night.

They told me today that my dad's partner wouldn't be going home to his child.

I saw he was a hero by the white roses painted blue and tied with his badge number.

I saw he was a hero by the way the people lined the streets.

I saw how he was a hero by the tears rolling down the cheeks of men, women, and children.

I saw how he was a hero with the riderless horse with the boots turned backward.

I heard he was a hero by the bagpipes playing "Amazing Grace."

I heard he was a hero by the silent arms that were presented by his fellow officers from all over the country as he was laid to rest.

My dad is a police officer. I don't have to be told—my dad is my true hero.